ER

Chorao, Kay
Lemon Moon

	DATE DUE	
FEB 1 8 1988	NOV	
APR 1 4 1988	AUG	
MAY 2		
M		

WDRAW

LEMON MOON

LEMON

written and illustrated by

MOON

KAY CHORAO

HOLIDAY HOUSE,
New York

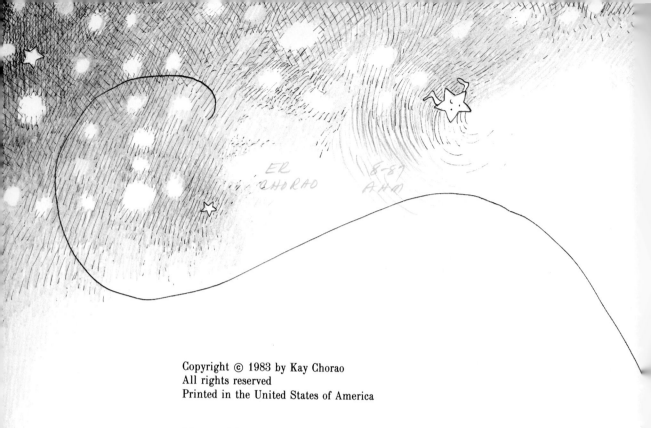

Library of Congress Cataloging in Publication Data

Chorao, Kay.
    Lemon moon.

    Summary: Grams has difficulty believing her grand-
child who is convinced that the moon grew stars and a
cat on a cloud ate the stars with a spoon.
    [1. Stories in rhyme. 2. Moon—Fiction. 3. Dreams—
Fiction] I. Title.
PZ8.3.C454Le 1983   [E]   83-220
ISBN 0-8234-0490-0

For Nellie Eby Fleming
and Ian .

rams said I dreamed it all.
Grams said I didn't fall.

"I sewed your quilt. I stitched it tight. Nothing flew around that night. The dogs are cotton, cut with shears. I sewed on floppy, velvet ears. There were never, ever bears."

But Grams never saw me jump
and leap, or heard me yell,

"I WILL

NOT SLEEP."

My feet made

everything fall free:

The dogs. The clouds. The bear. And me

Grams said she never sewed a moon.
And certainly not a moon balloon.
But the moon rose yellow in the air.
Grams said, "No!"
But it was there. . . .

And so was bear.

"Ouch," roared Bear, tumbling near.
"Don't keep leaping on my ear."

"No," said Grams, "it couldn't be."
"Oh, yes, it was. They jumped like me."

"With all your jumping we can't sleep," said one grumpy, woolly sheep.

The moon grew stars.
And they grew feet.
They danced in line,

A Starry Street.

"Nonsense," said Grams, when I told her that.

But then I remembered about the cat.

"A cat on a cloud ate stars with a spoon, while dogs and sheep tumbled by with the moon."

Grams laughed at me then.
She hugged me and said, "My silly, sweet silly, you have clouds in your head. My brain is too dusty, my bones just too rusty, but how I do wish I could join in your trip, and travel through space with a moon for a ship."

I smiled and I yawned and I said, "Good night."

Then Grams kissed me gently and turned off the light.

She tiptoed out and shut the door.
And the room was quieter than before.
But somewhere near my big left
toe, a lemon moon began to glow.